For all my readers. You're the best!

English translation by Marshall Yarbrough copyright © 2023 by Penguin Random House LLC

Das Kleine Böse Buch 3: Deine Zeit ist gekommen! text by Magnus Myst copyright © 2019 by Ueberreuter Verlag GmbH, Berlin
Cover art and interior illustrations by Thomas Hussung, copyright 2019 by Ueberreuter Verlag GmbH, Berlin

Visit us on the Web! rhcbooks.com

Educators and librarians, for a variety of teaching tools, visit us at RHTeachersLibrarians.com

Library of Congress Cataloging-in-Publication Data is available upon request.
ISBN 978-0-593-42767-5 (hardcover) — ISBN 978-0-593-42768-2 (ebook)

The text of this book is set in 16-point Adobe Jenson Pro.
Interior design by Cathy Bobak

MANUFACTURED IN ITALY
10 9 8 7 6 5 4 3 2 1
First American Edition

The Little Bad Book 3

YOUR TIME HAS COME!

By **MAGNUS MYST**

Illustrated by
Thomas Hussung

Translated by Marshall Yarbrough

Delacorte Press

Hey, you! Yeah, you! Glad you could finally make it! Oh man, where have you been this whole time? You are a reader, aren't you? You're not a robot from the future or some kind of caveman from the past? No, you're not either of those. You're totally a reader, right? Oh man, I hope so, because you see, I really need somebody who's got guts. And who is brave and clever and cunning and also, ideally, super-delicious!

Um, no, not delicious. **Forget I said that.** Brave and smart! That's what I wanted to say! That's totally enough!

Because the thing is, I really need your help! I can't tell you anything yet. But I promise you: if you play along, it won't just be super-exciting, it'll also be the last thing you ever . . . uh, I mean, the best time you've ever had! In your whole life! Honest! And that's because—get this—we're going to be . . .

Oh, no! Just a second. Hold on. There's one more thing I have to tell you: it could get just a tiny bit **DANGEROUS**. Or maybe more than just a tiny bit. And spooky, too. But you don't look like a scaredy-cat to me. You're brave enough to read me, right? Oh come on! Join me on page 14 and I'll tell you what this is all about.

—> KEEP READING ON PAGE 14 IF YOU WANT TO PLAY ALONG.

YOU KNOW WHERE YOU ARE?

The wrong
at the

place
wrong time!

QUICK, BACK TO PAGE 17,
OR YOU'LL BE

STUCK HERE FOREVER!

STOP!

Oh no, does this thing ever work? Where did we
end up this time?

And who are you?

Harhar! We're time pirates!

Wait, seriously? How cool! Real pirates?! The magic book told me about you.

So it is. We're time pirates. And we're going to steal time from you, harhar!

Sweet. And how do you do it? I mean, do you have a ship that you sail through time on? And cannons? Can we join you? Like, be part of your crew?

    I've stolen time from my readers before, and I like bad—

Quiet!

We're time pirates.
And time pirates steal time.

Yeah, fine, you said that already....

**When something takes a very,
veeeery, veeeeeeeeeeeeeeeeery
long time ... When your parents
say they're too busy for you, or
when something keeps repeating
over and over again or simply won't
end, or when you say Whoa, it's
THAT late already?! Then WE had
a hand in it! You'll find us lurking
in cell phones, in televisions, and in
books! We're simply everywhere!**

What? That's it?

You're not actually pirates? You're more like ...
time wasters? I thought it would be something
more exciting.

What a shame. All right then, so we'll just be leaving now, okay?

Oh, of course. As soon as we've stolen your time. Come on, hand it over! The only way you'll find out which page to turn to next is if you count all the x's on the next page. Have fun, harhar! And be sure to really take your time–no need to rush!

Oh no! Quick!

Harhar, har!!!

How mean! And what's the deal with this green 67? Why is that number here? Is that where we're supposed to turn next, maybe?

No, I don't know why the x's look like a 67. I'm afraid there's only one way out: you've got to count the x's! The total will tell us what page will lead us out of here.

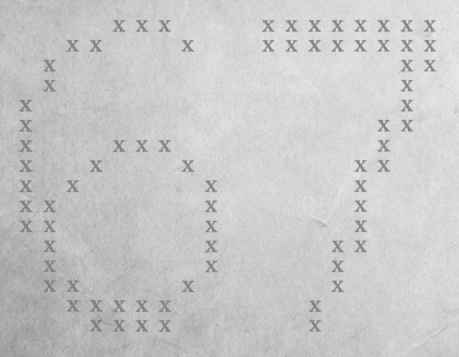

Okay, let's tell Perfecto's classmates a really awesome story, yeah? One that knocks their socks off. And I'll also teach them a few curse words, sort of on the side. They should learn something, after all, heeheehee.

The magic book did mention something about how one mustn't under any circumstances intervene in the time one travels to. But I mean, I'm just telling them a story. What could go wrong?

If they all end up getting eaten by the Time Wolf, so what?

Um. Uh, what did I just say? Time Wolf? What a joke. How did I ever come up with such nonsense? No, no, what I meant was: once Perfecto has read the end of the story, then we'll see. Yeah. Exactly. THAT'S what I was trying to say. You know what? I know a trick that'll let us fast-forward through time. Then we won't have to wait so long for Perfecto's class! It's just a little bit of magic, but it really works:

You see the drawing on the right? That's the Wheel of Time. It's driven by three cogs. But only one of them will turn it clockwise an hour into the future. The others will make the clock in the Wheel of Time turn backward and will only delay us.

INSIDE THE CORRECT COG IS THE PAGE NUMBER THAT WILL LET US TRAVEL AN HOUR INTO THE FUTURE.

So get going! The quicker you find it, the sooner we'll be there!

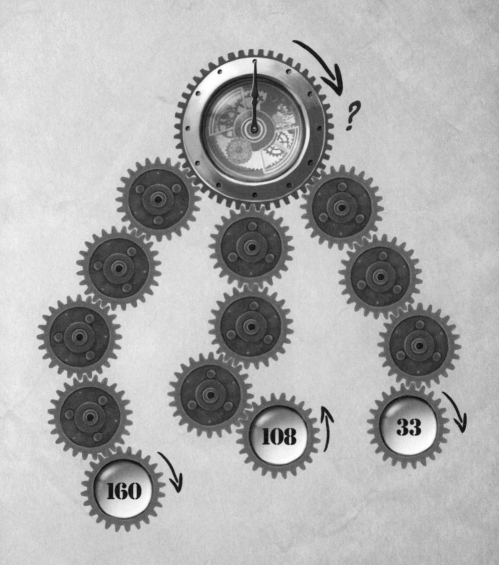

I knew it! You're in! Awesome! Okay, so let's talk. Here in my dungeon we're safe.

So: I'm the Little Bad Book. But if you think all I do is tell scary stories that make the blood in your veins run cold, you're wrong. Because believe it or not, this time I'm going to do something even better!

So a while ago, right? I was hanging out in this creepy castle. I thought if I poked around a little in the gloomy torture chambers, treasure vaults, and ruined watchtower, I might find some exciting stories. And way, way down in the crypt, I actually did find something!

Lying there with a whole bunch of coffins was an ancient book. It was hidden under a thick layer of dust. And the cover was half torn-off.

And suddenly it started talking to me! In a raspy voice, barely more than a whisper. It told me that it was a magic book and hadn't been read for three hundred years. And now that its ink had gotten really, really faded and it probably wouldn't ever find another reader again, it wanted to reveal to me its ancient secret. And that was . . . a magic spell that was hidden in its pages!

So I was super-excited, of course. I'm sure you can imagine! And then, once it had told me the magic spell, I was totally blown away. Because it was a magic spell for **TIME TRAVEL!**

Yes! Exactly! You read right! The book told me how to travel through time. Now I know how to do it!

And so I wanted to ask you: Do you want to come with me?

We can travel back to prehistoric times and fry up some dinosaur eggs for breakfast! Or we can go to the Stone Age, hand out matches to people, and watch them flip out and name us their chiefs! Or we can visit Mozart, play rock music for him, and hear what he has to say about it!

Or even better: We travel into the future! And we write down next week's lottery numbers! Awesome! Then we'll be rich. Oh yeah. Come on, let's do it!

I mean, only if you think you can handle it, of course.

Please, please! Do you want to? It'll be fun!

The old magic book did warn me a whole bunch of times that time travel was not something to be taken lightly, but I think I know why nobody reads his book anymore. I mean, what could go wrong? We're only having fun.

We just have to test you a little first. To make sure you've got what it takes to go time traveling. Not just anybody can do it, you know? It's a little like how only astronauts can fly to the moon. But you can figure it out, right?

I'm almost certain you'll be good at it. So, okay, if you've got what it takes to be a time traveler, then this question definitely won't be a problem for you:

IF YESTERDAY WAS MONDAY, WHAT DAY IS THE DAY AFTER TOMORROW?

TUESDAY —> KEEP READING ON PAGE 134.

SUNDAY —> KEEP READING ON PAGE 4.

THURSDAY —> KEEP READING ON PAGE 24.

HUH? —> KEEP READING ON PAGE 14.

STOP!

Halt! Stay where you are!

What? Did we really end up a thousand years in the future? And who are these dorks?

We are not dorks! We are the Time Police! Here. Our badge:

Time Police? Never heard of 'em. What's your deal?

We make sure that things move from beginning to end and not the other way around. We protect the flow of time. Which you three are making a mess of! Stop jumping through time at once! If you keep it up, the whole universe could explode!

Oh, don't worry. We'll be careful.

YOU'LL be careful?! You've already introduced several logical glitches! And far worse than that, you've awakened the Time Wo . . .

Whoa whoa whoa! What do we care

about logic? Who needs it! Now leave us alone already. You're all talk, anyway.

Dear reader of this book, listen closely: put this book aside and stow it in a secure location. Quickly! It's dangerous! You're in mortal peril!

You're just yanking our chain! "Mortal peril," pssh. Just because we're doing a little time traveling? It's fun!

So come on, you two.

Let's get out of here.

This time let's really make an effort, all right? I'd like to hear a really loud BING-BANG-BONG.

If you resist, we'll have to arrest you.

Let's go, quick! Away from here! Far off into the future, th_t w_y we . . . th_t w_y we! Oh no, now my little _ is missing! Wh_t's going on here? I need th_t! _bsolutely! _! _! _! _! _____ aaaaaaaaaa!!!

Ah, thank goodness, there it is again.

That's a clear sign! The lost "a" shows that the Tooth of Time is gnawing on you, because the Time Wo . . .

Nonsense! Stop scaring my readers. And you call yourself the police.

Quick! Let's hide in my dungeon! *I'LL ENCRYPT THE PAGE WITH A QUESTION THAT ONLY YOU TWO CAN ANSWER.* That way we can get rid of these spoilsports.

WHAT IS THE FINAL, SECRET INGREDIENT IN THE COLA RECIPE?

COUGH MEDICINE = 71

EARWAX = 21

COMPOST LIQUID = 38

THE RIGHT INGREDIENT TELLS YOU WHERE
TO FIND US.

The Time Police will never find us there!

LOOGIES = 74

SALT = 3

SPIDERS = 64

BOOGERS = 15

OLD BATTERIES = 45

Hey! You did it! Thursday! Duh. Wow! I always knew there was a good time traveler hidden in you somewhere.

But don't get too excited! Real time traveling isn't easy. That's why you really must do a few things to prepare. They're very important, the magic book says.

First, you'll need a **Time Travel Emergency Kit**. It's kind of like survival gear—you know, just in case something goes wrong.

 Gather all your favorite **sweets**. Not only is it good to always have an emergency supply, they're also great for trading or using as bait in the Stone Age and medieval times.

You also need a big **towel.** You can use it as a coat, a picnic blanket, a sunshade, a bedsheet, a tent—or, of course, as a towel.

 Do you have a **watch?** Then go get it! It doesn't matter what kind. Just don't lose it, whatever you do! It'll always show you where we are in time at any particular moment.

 The last thing you need is a **Band-Aid.** For emergencies. Nothing bad is going to happen, I promise. But the magic book said it's super-important, so just go grab one real quick, okay?

Now pack it all up in a bag.

I'll wait here till you're finished.

Have you got it all? Then read on!

Actually, just two more little details . . .

First, look at your watch and **READ THE TIME.**

That's our time anchor, you understand? This way we'll always know when our journey began. **Use a piece of your own paper and note the time and date that you will start your time journey.**

Very good. And now, the very last thing I need is your signature. Also on that piece of paper, copy the statement below and sign your name.

> **I, the reader of this book, swear to take responsibility for everything that happens, even if I get swallowed by a time vortex, I create unsolvable glitches in logic, or I get eaten by a giant, terrifying, evil wolf. Signed:**

Don't worry. This is just for ... uh ... for your own safety.

Once you've filled everything out, you just have to make it through one last safety check.

This clock shows the next page number in military time. **AS SOON AS YOU'VE FOUND OUT WHAT IT IS, TURN TO THAT PAGE.** That way I'll know that you can actually tell time. The little cog will help you if you need a hint.

Huh?! This isn't the future, is it? What is this place?

Oh, this must be a **time vortex!** The old magic book talked a whole lot about these. This is where different time lines run together. We just have to follow our own line, and then we'll come out on

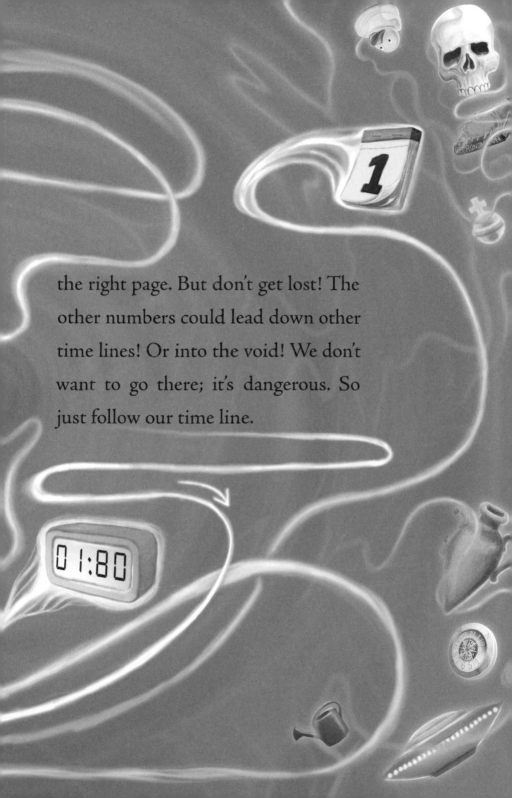

the right page. But don't get lost! The other numbers could lead down other time lines! Or into the void! We don't want to go there; it's dangerous. So just follow our time line.

Very good! 00:30, which is military time, for those in the know. The 12 is also a 0! That was big. Now I know you're ready for our first *TIME JUMP!*

Are you as excited as I am?

That reminds me: we still have to decide where we want to go.

You know what? As a little test, let's just jump a hundred years into the future, okay?

I'll show you how it works:

You see the magic drawing on the page after next? That's our time machine! Yes, really!

Way at the bottom you'll see the number of years we're jumping into the future. A hundred years. That should be enough for now.

The clock on the left shows our **time line number.**

And the clock on the right is our **chro-nometer.** No idea what that means. All that matters is that you follow these steps:

1. **Add together the time line number and the number on the chronometer.**

2. **Put your finger in the middle. Right there where the wormhole is.**

3. **In a really loud voice, say: TICK-TOCK-TICK-TOCK-BING-BANG-BONG!**

4. **Shake your head and call out the sum from step one.**

If you've done everything correctly, the number you're calling out will appear in the space at the top. You'll actually be able to see it! That's the secret magic at work. If everything lines up, we'll turn to the page we've calculated and hop on into the future.

Got it? Then let's go!

Oh man, if this really works, we'll see each

other again in a hundred years! How sweet is that?! So don't forget:

ADD THE TIME LINE NUMBER AND CHRONOMETER READING TOGETHER, PUT YOUR FINGER ON THE WORMHOLE, SHAKE YOUR HEAD, AND CALL OUT TICK-TOCK-TICK-TOCK-BING-BANG-BONG AND THE NUMBER YOU'VE CALCULATED! THEN YOU'LL SEE WHAT PAGE THE FUTURE AWAITS US ON!

Sweet! The fast-forwarding worked! You make a really great time traveler. You're really a super reader!

Now we just need Perfecto. Is he here already? Perfecto? Hello?

Yes, hello, here I am! My teacher thinks it's a great idea for me to read a story out of you to the class. She even connected a few other classes. Now they're all listening, too! And they're really excited already. So am I. Is it true that people in the twenty-first century wasted lots and

lots of time sleeping? And that they
got runny noses? And how exactly did
this "money" thing work?

Yes, the century I come from is indeed a dark time,
true. People still lie in bed at night, not doing
anything, just dreaming; snot and boogers drip
from their noses when they get colds; and they're
always fighting over money. And even if we do
still eat sweets, life here is certainly no cakewalk.

To show you all how things are in our time,
I'll tell you the story of Lexi, a girl to whom Fate
dealt a particularly cruel hand. Sure, she was a
happy, nice girl. But sadly, she had one big problem: for you see, she was ugly.

What? You still had that kind of thing
back then? Could parents not pick what
their kids would look like yet?

No, it was still totally up to chance. And so from Lexi's head sprouted a wild tangle of frizzy hair that no brush could tame. Because one of her eyeteeth was crooked, she had to wear braces. And on top of that, she had a liver spot on her nose. It was very small, but whenever she saw it in the mirror, it seemed to her gigantic. She hated it with all her heart. She even hated the words "liver spot." Bleh!

Lexi didn't think it was fair. She'd never done anything bad or mean. Why couldn't she be as beautiful as the Starlets?

The Starlets were three girls in her class who were mega pretty. Everyone admired them. Lexi hardly dared to even speak to them,

35

she was so intimidated. But one day she looked in the mirror and her hair was yet again standing up in every direction like she'd been struck by lightning, and finally she'd had all she could take. She summoned all her courage and asked the three girls to tell her the secret of their beauty. Did they eat anything in particular? Did they use an expensive cream? Or a secret shampoo?

The three Starlets looked at her in surprise. But then Tiffany smiled her perfect smile, brushed her hair behind her ear, and said, "I actually do know a trick that'll work for you: Just

put a paper bag over your head. Then your face will immediately look prettier."

She smiled at Lexi with her glowing white teeth, and the other two Starlets laughed.

Lexi stood there frozen for a second, and just barely managed to turn around and run away before the tears came. She needed a place to hide, so she locked herself in a stall in the girls' bathroom. Rage simmered like tomato sauce inside her. That was so mean! Why couldn't she be beautiful? And why was beauty given instead to those three . . . those three . . .

Suddenly, her head was filled with countless foul, unflattering, unspeakable words. And then she realized which of them would best suit the Starlets. And she got out a pencil and scribbled three stick figures on the stall door, and beneath it, channeling all her rage, she wrote the fitting insult.

Hey, I've got an idea! Perfecto? You all can guess it. What did she call the three of them? This way you'll learn something about curse words from the twenty-first century. Sweet, huh? History class should always be like this.

So, **WHAT DID SHE WRITE ON THE STALL DOOR?** What did she call the three Starlets? For you, dear reader, this shouldn't be a problem—you certainly know your way around the twenty-first century!

 Sluggy Slowpokes ⟶ *PAGE 35*

 Stuck-Up Little Prissy Misses ⟶ *PAGE 57*

 Cowardly Crybabies ⟶ *PAGE 163*

Okay, fine, I'll admit it: no wars and no sickness—that sounds all right. And a 4D gaming console would of course be insane. But that's totally nuts, right? I mean, they're using it to play golf! And they don't have books anymore. And the Goggle keeps watch over everything they hear and say!

I'll bet Perfecto would like to have fun. He just doesn't know what fun is. Listen, here's what we'll do:

I'll tell them a funny story. And if Perfecto laughs, then we'll know that there's still hope for humanity. And if not, we'll just let them keep on being boring and jump to a more exciting time.

Deal? *KEEP READING ON PAGE 11.*

Yeah! I knew it. You see things the same way I do.

I mean, how can you have a 4D video game console and just play golf with it? And only ever do what you're told all the time? That's just horrible! And they don't eat sweets anymore! Can you imagine?

Luckily, you've got an emergency supply in your time-travel kit. You still have your kit with you, don't you? Now you see how important it is! If you don't, you'd better go get it real quick: sweets, towel, watch, and Band-Aid. Looks like the magic book wasn't joking when it said we'd need these things when time traveling. . . .

Hey, listen, should we mess with them a little? Come on, I know just the thing. We'll tell them a story that really floors them. By the end of it, their mouths will be hanging open. Then they'll find out what fun really means. Heeheehee.

Are you up for it?

THEN KEEP READING ON PAGE 11.

What did you do? We're in the VOID! This isn't where we want to be! Quick, back to page 103!

Hey, you did it! Wasn't hard finding the things that tell time, was it?

And Perfecto? Did he figure it out, too?

Yes, here I am! I solved your time-travel puzzle! Does that mean I get to come with you?

Nice. Maybe you're not such a hopeless case after all. But remember: You must do exactly as I tell you. And you need a time-travel kit. So get yourself something to eat, a towel, a watch, and most important of all, a Band-Aid.

I got an A in obedience! I can handle it. I'll go right now and get everything.

They give you grades for obedience? Ugh, maybe we really were doing those future dweebs a favor by stirring things up a bit.

All right, once Perfecto has everything, we can continue our journey. Let's jump through time again, yeah? Let's say . . . a thousand years into the future? There's something I just have to show you two!

Oh yeah! Maybe the people a thousand years from now will have made contact with extraterrestrials. Or they'll have super-intelligent computers with mind control.

Yeah. Exactly. Really exciting, isn't it? That's just what we're about to find out. So let's go, then. You know what to do, dear reader. Here it is once more for Perfecto:

45

ADD THE TIME LINE NUMBER AND THE
CHRONOMETER READING DISPLAYED ON THE
TIME MACHINE'S TWO CLOCKS AND PUT YOUR
FINGER ON THE WORMHOLE. AND THEN SAY
OUT LOUD: TICK-TOCK-TICK-TOCK-
BING-BANG-BONG! AND SHAKE YOUR
HEAD WHILE YOU'RE DOING IT!

When the number you've calculated appears in the field at the top, then you'll know what page to turn to in order to make our leap into the future.

So get to it! We'll see each other in a thousand years!

Yes! We're out of the time vortex! Sweet! Okay. How's it looking? Did the time jump work? Are we a hundred years in the future?

Go look out the window! Are there any flying cars up in the sky? Or robot dogs running around in the street? And what does your watch say?

What?

Nothing happened? Are you sure?

Hmm.

I don't get it. How come it didn't work? Did you say the magic spell really loudly? I planned it all out exactly so that we would run into the Time Wo ... uh, I mean, come out in the future. Crap. What went wrong?

Hello! What are you? You can talk!

What? Who? Now, listen, what kind of question is that? I'm the Little Bad Book. It's written right there on my cover.

Oh neat. My name's Perfecto. I just found you in a box in my grandparents' attic. What's a book?

Excuse me? You don't know what a book is?!

No, I've never seen anything like you. What are books for? Where's your On button? How long do your batteries last? And why are you so ugly?

UGLY?! Listen, kid, have you got a screw loose or something?! You think you're perfect, is that it? Where did you come from, anyway?

I'm from the year 2120. And of course I'm perfect. My parents ordered me that way; I don't have any defects. Every day my Super-Mega-Hyper-Goggle tells me what to eat and how much exercise to do so that I can optimize my development. Is that not how it is with you?

Ha! I knew it. The magic spell did work! At least a little bit. You're a reader from the future! Tell me, what's it like there? Do you have cities on the moon? Do your shoes tie themselves? Oh, and one thing I absolutely have to know: What kind of curse words do you have?

Curse words?! Shhh! Watch out. They're forbidden. I can't believe you don't know that.

Forbidden?!

My Super-Mega-Hyper-Goggle in my eye constantly monitors what I hear and see. That way I don't come into contact with anything that isn't good for me.

But . . . can I tell you something? I know one anyway! Should I say it?

Duh! That's what books are there for, you know. To teach people things. So come on! Let's have it!

All right. But I have to cover up the Goggle, or else I'll get bad grades. Brace yourself:

Hey, you clamshell!

Hee, hee, totally twixi, right?

What?!

Hold on—that was it? "Clamshell"? THAT'S supposed to be a *CURSE WORD?!* But ... but ...

That won't do AT ALL! That's totally boring!

Did there used to be worse curse words? Oh my, those must have been scary times. I've heard about the twenty-first century in history class. Is it true that people used to get sick back then? And that there were wars? And that they ate sugar?

WHAT?! You don't have sugar anymore?

Of course not. Sugar has been forbidden for a long time. I've heard that when you eat it, your teeth immediately fall out and you puff up all big and round like a balloon. You'd know that, though, if you'd completed your learning units. You really are a strange book.

Yeah, but you must do *something* to have fun! Do you have parties? Or tell jokes?

Jokes?! It's not appropriate to laugh at other people. But of course we have fun. Sometimes my friends and I get together to play 4D Super-Golf. It's totally rad. You can actually feel the wind on your skin!

Excuse me? You have computer games where you can actually feel the wind—and you use them to play golf?!

Man, are you old-fashioned. Golf is hypertwixi! You really must be from the past. You have no idea what's twixi.

Hey, listen, can I take you to school with me for show-and-tell? My teacher would definitely like that. I'm sure we can learn a lot from you about the mistakes of the past.

MISTAKES?! Hey, are you nuts?!

All right, fine. I'll just put you back in the box, then.

No, uh, wait! Hold on!
I meant to say, um . . .
All right, why not?
Of course you can take me to school. That's a

great idea. I promise to tell an especially infor-mative story. Promise. You just have to turn to page 33 as soon as you get to school, okay?

I'll wait here in the meantime.

Oh super! I'll definitely get an A for this! See you soon!

Phew. Is he gone?

Good. But you, dear reader, you're still here, right? **THEN LET'S GO TO PAGE 166** for a second, okay? There's something I have to talk to you about.

What, you really had such sweet insults in the past? My teacher said that was certainly very informative, but no more, please, okay? Lots of kids' Goggles have started beeping already!

Yes, now you all can see how bad things were in the twenty-first century. And it got way, way worse. For just as Lexi started writing, the Starlets came into the bathroom. To her amazement, they were looking for her!

It was like this, Eva whispered to her excitedly from the other side of the stall door. The truth was, they really did know a secret! But they couldn't tell it to her at school. If they did, people would think they were witches! Because the secret of their beauty had to do with magic. Yes, really! Or to be more specific: with a magic potion.

Curious, Lexi opened the door and listened.

Whoever drank this magic potion would become beautiful forever.

"Here's the recipe," said Eva, and put a piece of paper in Lexi's hand. "Brew the potion tonight and bring it tomorrow morning at recess. Then we'll add the last, secret ingredient. And when you drink it, you'll be as beautiful as we are, forever."

With that, they left Lexi in the bathroom. In her hand she held the recipe.

A magic potion? That made you beautiful forever? Could she believe them? Should she? Maybe they were just trying to play a trick on her.

But then she imagined how great it would be if

her hair didn't always lead a life of its own. And if everyone she met liked her at first glance. And then she knew: there was only one way to find out whether all they'd said was true. She had to give this potion a try.

Luckily, her parents went to bed early that evening. She was able to sneak into the kitchen and tiptoe around preparing the potion. The recipe was simple: "Put the seven grossest things you can think of in a pot, fill it with old dishwater, and boil for an hour, stirring constantly. The grosser the ingredients, the more potent the potion."

Lexi stared with disgust as a moldy apple with a worm inside it sank into the pot of dishwater. It was followed by an old sock and a handful of dead spiders she'd found in the basement. After that, she poured in a cup of the smelly liquid she'd collected from the bottom of the compost bin. Immediately, the pot started to bubble, and green steam rose from it. She bravely clamped her nostrils with a clothespin and kept at it. All that was missing to round the whole thing off was a good helping of earwax, one wet booger, and one turnip. When she put the turnip in, she couldn't help but gag, nose clip or no nose clip.

Again she started to have doubts. Even if the

Starlets were telling her the truth, would she be able to swallow this disgusting brew? She shivered at the thought.

But then she pictured again how great it would be to finally be beautiful. And she smiled and stirred.

That night she could hardly sleep. And when she met the Starlets in the girls' bathroom again the next day and they admired the plastic bottle full of black bubbling liquid she'd brought, she immediately blurted out, "Will you tell me the secret ingredient now? Please!"

"Sure," said Tiffany, and tried to suppress a giggle. "It's the most important one of all. You know that the grosser the potion is, the more potent it is. That's why . . ."

And with those words, Tiffany opened the bottle, and Lexi watched as she noisily hocked up a giant loogie and spit it into the bottle.

Ashley and Eva stepped up to the bottle and followed her example, giggling as they did so.

Lexi felt sick. She gulped. And then the disaster happened.

After the last loogie made it into the bottle, it began to fizz like crazy! Eva tried to cover it with her hand and immediately started screaming. But the brew just kept getting fizzier and fizzier! Ashley tried to put the top back on, but it was too late—the pressure was too great. Suddenly, a giant stream of liquid sprayed from under Eva's hand with a loud hiss. Like a rocket, the bottle flew this way and that across the room and sprayed everything around it: The mirror. The ceiling. The floor. Even the tips of the Starlets' noses were dripping with sticky black liquid.

It was so nasty that Lexi started gagging again and covered her face with her hands!

Hey, wait a second, what kind of story is this? My teacher says I should stop reading right now! Some of us here are already sick! And my Goggle keeps beeping nonstop!

Sorry. I'm not making this up, you know. I'm just telling you what happened. This is just what the twenty-first century was like. But don't worry, here comes the most important part! You can't miss it!

When Lexi finally took her hands from her face, she could barely believe her eyes: the Starlets were licking the black brew from their lips and even lapping it up from puddles on the floor!

Instead of the gross drink that the Starlets wanted her to make—they really were just trying to prank her—Lexi had by total coincidence discovered the secret recipe for a sweet sugary beverage that everyone in the twenty-first century knew and loved: cola.

Hello?

Perfecto?

Hello, are we alone here? Helloooo?

HA!

You see? Just like I thought. It's nothing but boring dorks in the future.

Fine. If Perfecto's not game, we'll just forget it. Let's ditch this bogus future. We'll try another time jump. We've got to start making our way to the Time Wo . . .

Um. I mean, somewhere else . . . Come on!

We'll travel to ancient Rome and snatch the laurels off Caesar's head!

Or better yet, we'll visit your parents in the past, and then you can tell them that we come from the future and that a zombie virus is going to be unleashed and you're the only person who can stop the disease from wreaking havoc. But only if they raise your allowance; otherwise all is lost! It'll be tons of fun! Just picture the looks on their faces!

COME ON, LET'S DO IT. FOLLOW ME TO PAGE 68!

Harhar,

Bet you thought you were reaa

Thanks so muc

. . . that you've gone and
frittered away here,
harhar!

al clever!

n for the time

Go back to page 10 . . .

and count up all those x's like a good reader,
or else you'll never get out of here!

How could you tell such a horrible story? That was not twixi! Because of you I had to go to the principal's office and got a bad grade!

Oh, Perfecto! There you are. What's that? Just for reading a story? HA! Well, there you have it. Just goes to show you how unfair things are where you come from. I mean, it was a joke.

A joke? That wasn't funny! Poor Lexi!

What do you mean, poor? I don't know what your problem is. That was a happy ending.

What could possibly be happy about it?
The girls' bathroom was wrecked. Everybody had to drink that nasty drink. And
in the end Lexi was still . . . still
had crooked teeth.

Man, you really didn't get it, did you? Because Lexi
now knew the secret recipe for cola, she became
incredibly rich. Makes sense, right? And
so she threw lots of parties, had lots of friends,
and lived a life of luxury and ease! She went from
frizzy hair to fizzy fame and fortune! Heh heh.
And hey, her braces came off eventually.

Are you trying to say that everything
turned out fine because in the end that
revolting stuff made her rich? That's
even worse!

Why are you even here if all you're going to do is complain? If you don't like it, stop reading.

Because . . . well . . . because I want to know what else you've got to tell. I've never heard a story like that before.

Does that mean you thought it was fun?

Wait, I have to cover my Goggle for a second. . . .
So . . . um . . . well, okay, maybe a little.

Haha! I knew it! That's 'cause my stories are the absolute best! I'm the Little Bad Book, baby! And soon enough I'll be a Big Bad Book, haha!

But if you really want to play along, there's something you have to prepare yourself for. See, this time I'm not just telling funny stories. This time we're traveling through time!

What? Time travel? Seriously? Isn't that dangerous?

Sure it is. But hey, we're being careful. Plus we've got a Band-Aid with us. And so far everything's been fine. What co_ld go wrong, anyway?

H_h? What was that? How come all of a s_ dden I can't say _ anymore? _._!_____!_!_!_! _!!! _ndergro_nd. _mbrella. Underpants!

Ha! Haha, there it is again. U! U, u, u! Phew! All right, then.

Hmm. Strange. What was that? Oh well, whatever.

Can I come with you? Seriously, that would be hyper-twixi!

Hmm. They do say two readers are better than one. But I don't know. . . . First I have to test you to see if you've got what it takes to be a time traveler. Okay, here's how we'll do it:

Look at the dots on the right. **SOME OF THESE THINGS CAN TELL TIME. IF YOU CAN MANAGE TO FIND ALL OF THEM AND LINK THEM TOGETHER IN ALPHABETICAL ORDER, THEY'LL SHOW YOU THE NUMBER OF THE PAGE WHERE THE STORY CONTINUES**—and then you can come! For you, dear reader, this will be no problem, I mean, you've already passed all the other tests:

WHICH PAGE NUMBER IS ENCIRCLED WHEN YOU CONNECT THE CORRECT ANSWERS IN ALPHABETICAL ORDER?

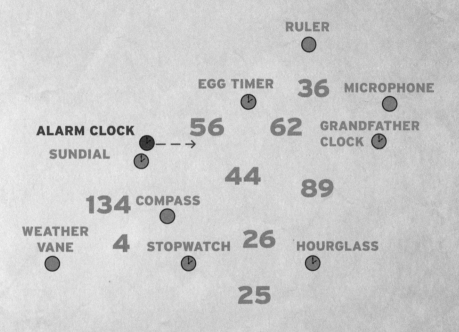

Yes! We escaped! **Phew,** who WERE those dweebs? I don't know what their problem is.

But they said they're the police! You're supposed to listen to the police.

Oh, come on, those weren't real police officers. No, no. "Time Police"? Anybody could say that. In reality I'm sure they were just . . . umm . . . time pirates! Exactly. Pirates who wanted to steal time from us. The magic book warned me specifically about them. We can count ourselves lucky we got away from them.

Come on. Let's finally go see what's happening a thousand years from now. I'm so excited to find out!

You know how it works, right?

1. ADD THE TIME LINE NUMBER ON THE LEFT AND THE CHRONOMETER READING ON THE RIGHT AND PUT YOUR FINGER ON THE WORMHOLE.

2. SHOUT TICK-TOCK-TICK-TOCK-BING-BANG-BONG AND SHAKE YOUR HEAD.

3. JUMP TO THE PAGE THAT APPEARS IN THE FIELD AT THE TOP.

Come
see us
again!

6

Oh no! We're back in the time vortex!
One of these wormholes is bound to lead
us out of here. But which one?

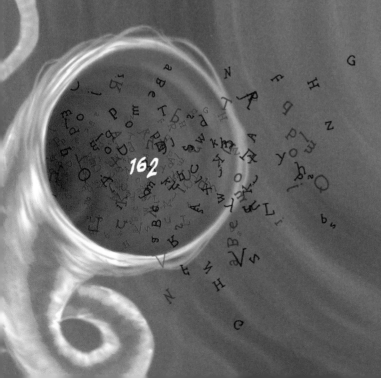

162

What do you think the deal is with
the multicolored question marks
in that wormhole down there?

One of the question marks is green. . . .
Weren't the pirates' x's all in the shape of
a green number? Maybe that has something to do with it?

?+?+? =

PAGE NUMBER

Huh? Very weird. Where are we now?

Hey! Aren't those . . . I think those
are atoms! But atoms are incredibly
small! How come we can see them?

We wanted to go to the future, not the
microcosmos! What's going on?

Just look at this place. I think that
stuff on the edges is quantum foam!
I've heard about it at school. Hey,
and that thing over there? Is that a
number? A pink 42? And over there—

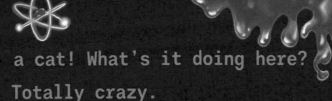

a cat! What's it doing here?
Totally crazy.

All right, something's wrong with the magic spell.
Maybe the magic book gave me the wrong one?
Or ... Oh no! I hope what happened to that boy
doesn't happen to us.

What boy?

Oh ... it's not important.

Oh, come on, tell us.

All right, fine. But you guys have to promise me
you won't panic.

Um, I can't promise anything . . . but
I'll try not to.

Good. Okay, so once there was a boy named Max. He was a brilliant inventor.

He even won a prize for one of his inventions, an automatic pineapple peeler. But he wanted to

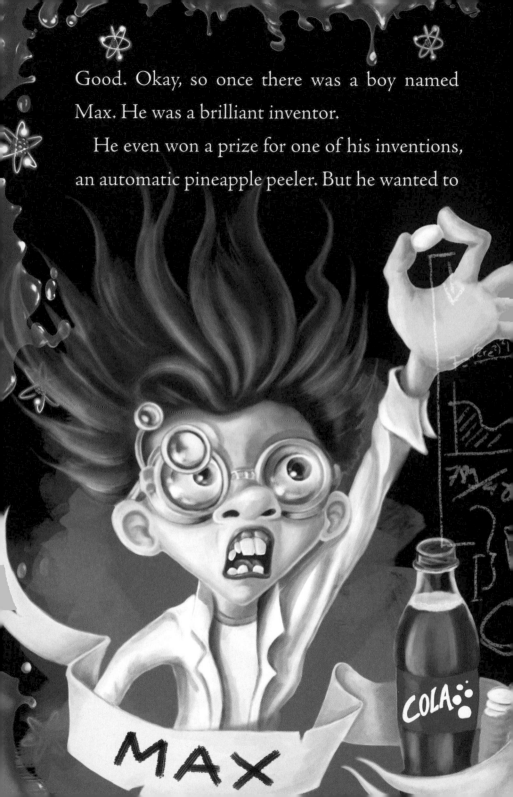

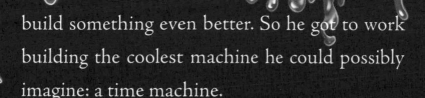

build something even better. So he got to work building the coolest machine he could possibly imagine: a time machine.

After weeks of tinkering in his basement workshop, he managed to build a prototype using a microwave, a laser pointer, and two mirrors. Of course, this wasn't as clever as what we're doing here with magic and incantations. His machine could only travel a few days into the past. And only for five minutes—then he had to go back. But that was enough for him.

On his first test run, he managed to smuggle into the past a piece of paper with the questions from the previous week's English quiz.

He *hated* English! When he got back and looked at his grade, he saw that he'd earned an A+! The machine really worked!

It wasn't five minutes before he climbed back into the machine and warned himself about the "lemon" candy that Lisa was going to offer him on Friday after chemistry class. It had been so sour that he had burst into tears in front of the whole class and somebody had scribbled "crybaby" on his book bag.

When he came back from this second time jump, the words were gone!

He was thrilled. His time machine was the coolest invention he'd ever come up with. From now on, he could reverse every mistake he made! Simply brilliant!

Meanwhile, it didn't bother him that his book bag was a different color now that the scribbled words had disappeared. And as for the scar that showed up on the back of his hand after he improved his English grade, he barely paid it any

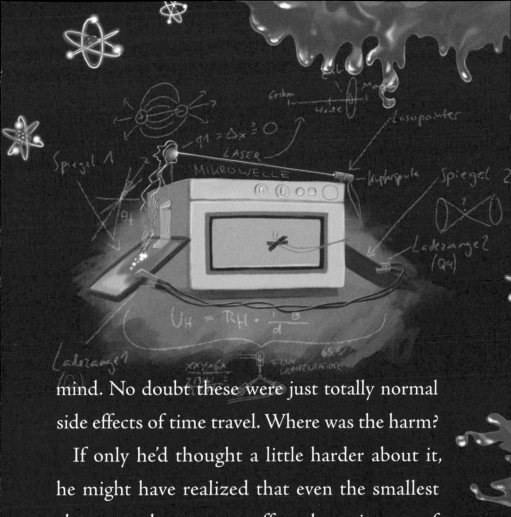

mind. No doubt these were just totally normal side effects of time travel. Where was the harm?

If only he'd thought a little harder about it, he might have realized that even the smallest change to the past can affect the trajectory of the future. Like a snowflake that triggers an avalanche, or a butterfly that flaps its wings and changes the course of history. In the same way, Max's time jumps changed the world's sequence of events in a way that was totally out of control.

But because Max didn't know this, he was already getting excited about his next brilliant plan.

The following evening he smuggled into the past a small slip of paper on which was written the winning numbers for a lottery drawing. The prize was a dream house. And as soon as he got back from his time jump and ran to the living room, he saw his whole family there celebrating in front of the TV.

It took until the day after Wednesday for Max to realize that something wasn't right. All of a sudden it was Friday. Where had Thursday gone? Nobody had ever heard of this day!

Max started to feel a bit uneasy. So even though a missing Thursday wasn't exactly a catastrophe, he promised himself that he would only travel to the past in emergencies.

Unfortunately, just such an emergency arose a few days later, when his mother fell from a rickety ladder and broke her leg. Max had to do something about that, didn't he? And so yet again he turned on the machine and traveled back to the past, then tightened the ladder's loose screw.

Oh, if only he hadn't done it! When he got back, his mother was doing great again. But suddenly, everyone was speaking a foreign language! And only after a while did he realize that they were speaking backward!

Oh no! This couldn't be! What had he done? Things were getting worse and worse.

He started thinking frantically. Immediately, he came up with an idea that would fix everything: if he could stop himself from inventing the time machine, then none of this would ever happen and everything would be good again.

Since he could only travel a few days at a time into the past, he wrote a note:

"Dear Max, Don't build a time machine, whatever you do. It ends badly. Please keep passing this note deeper into the past until it reaches a Max who doesn't have a time machine yet. Yours, Future Max."

He anxiously handed the note to his past self. And that self handed it to another Max deeper in the past. And so on.

But this time when Max came back from the past, everything had only gotten worse. Sure, his family was speaking forward again. And Thursdays were back. But everybody's ears, noses, and feet were gigantic!

Max was desperate. He needed more energy!
So for his next attempt, he linked all the elec-
trical outlets in the house with extension cords.

The machine hummed ominously and started smoking. But this didn't help, either: when he got back, everybody was just running around naked! Max tried even more new tricks in his efforts to put the world back in order. But after his next attempt, his parents were suddenly robots! And after the next try, the whole world was made of nothing but pink cotton candy! It seemed like nothing would bring back the good old times. And there the story ends. Still, Max wanders in search of his family. He has never found, never finds, and never will find his old home.

Oh no. That's horrible! The poor guy!

Yes, I admit, it's not a pretty story. Still, I don't think—I mean, I'm almost certain that it has nothing whatsoever to do with us.

But isn't that exactly what
we're doing? Traveling through time?

Nonsense. We're using magic, duh. That's
completely different. Nothing bad can happen
to us.

I don't know. I've got a bad feeling
about this.

Trust me. Nothing bad is going to happen.
But if it'll make you two feel better, we can
do a little test to see if you're still living in
your world or if you've slipped into a different time line.

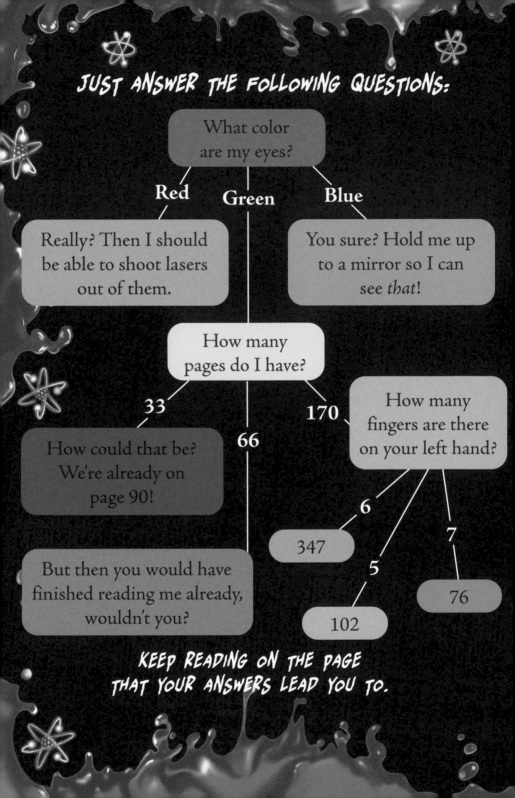

Hello?

Hellooo?!

Hey, where did the Little Bad Book go? How come it's not saying anything?

This can't be happening. Hello?

HEEELLLOOOOOOOOO?!

Oh man! Not twixi. Not at all twixi!

But you're still there, right? The reader from the twenty-first century?

Phew. At least there's that.

Oh no. If the Little Bad Book isn't here, what are we supposed to do? What do you do when there's no one to tell you what to do?

Aaaah, I don't know! I'm feeling

very light-headed. I have to sit down for a second.

Easy, now. Deep breaths. Phewwwww . . .

Oh man, I knew it! I never should have come! The Time Police clearly warned us that the Little Bad Book was dangerous.

Why did it just leave us on our own like this? Why would it do such a thing?!

Hello!? Where are you?! HELLOOO?!

Oh no, I have to distract myself. Or else I'll go crazy.

Can I ask you something?

Are you really from the twenty-first century? What's it like there? In your time?

It must be way scary, right? I've heard there were people who had to wear glasses. And did you really only live to be a hundred years old? And . . . and what was the deal with those cell phones? Did you really not have a Goggle in your eye to look after you and tell you what to do?

You must be mega brave if you can handle all that. I think I would flip out.

Oh man, the book still isn't here. Where could it be? What should we do now?

Do you think it's up to something?

Do you know what I did once? I tried a piece of candy. My classmate Astra brought it to school. And then at recess we licked it in secret.

At first I was too afraid to do it.

But then it was super sweet! I'd never tasted anything that sweet in my whole life. And weirdly enough, my teeth didn't fall out. . . .

Am I bad now?

I don't know. Is there anything you really like that you're actually not supposed to do, but you do it anyway? In secret?

Oh, shame. I'd really like to know. But of course I can't hear you.

Although . . . wait a second! You could write it down! Yeah, exactly! Then I'll see it a hundred years from now. Kind of like a message from the past!

Oh yeah! Should we give it a try?

Is there anything that's against the rules that you think is fun?

Just write it down on a piece of paper. Don't worry, I'm able to read it.

SERIOUSLY?! Whoa, you're really . . .

Oh man! Ohmanohmanohman! There you are, finally! Where were you two? I thought I'd lost you!

We were waiting for you! You ditched us!

Whaaat? No, that's not at all true. I would never do something like that! It's just . . . this time it really worked! I traveled through time! After you two said the spell, I suddenly found myself standing in a clearing in a green forest. The sun was shining. Behind me was a big mountain, and above me was a clear blue sky. Everything was calm and peaceful.

Green everywhere? Blue sky? Great!
Does that mean people a thousand
years from now live in harmony with
nature? That would be totally wonderful!

I thought so, too. But when I looked around,
there was no sign of people anywhere. No
spaceships or cities in the clouds. Not even a
hut.

Then I heard something. Kind of a growl.
It got louder and louder, until the whole
ground trembled! All of a sudden there was a
BANG. I've never heard anything so loud.
And then I saw it: the mountain. It was a
volcano—and it had erupted!

Everything was shaking, and a column of fire shot way up into the sky and started falling back down—right where I was standing! Suddenly, all these dinosaurs came running out of the forest. They just stampeded right over me because they were fleeing from the explosion!

And then I knew that something still wasn't right with the magic spell. I wasn't in the future, I was in the past—not a thousand years back but 60 million. And I wanted to get out of there as fast as I could!

Seriously, now? You're not making this up?

Making it up?! Meee? Check **THIS** out!
I almost lost a whole page because a Brachiosaurus came and stomped all over me before I could say the magic spell.

Wow, you sure got lucky.

You're telling me! Time travel is really _____!

Oh no, what's wrong now? Did you two see that? I've lost a whole word all of a sudden!

That is not good. Not _____ at all. He's getting closer! We have to hurry!

Who's getting closer?

Um, no one. Doesn't matter. Let's go. Come on. We'll try it again. But _____ some effort into it, all right? We want to travel to the distant future. You have to say the TICK-TOCK-TICK-TOCK-BING-BANG-BONG really loudly or something will go wrong again. I'm counting on you!

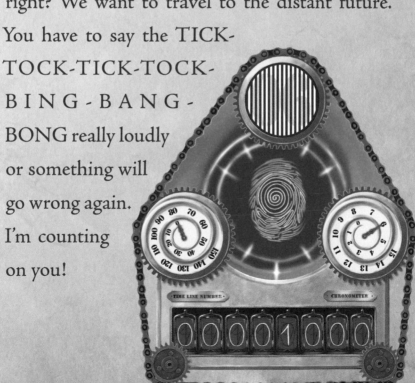

Right! My eyes are green. I have 170 pages. And you've got seven fingers on your hand. Wait a minute . . . Whatwhatwhat? You've got FIVE fingers on your hand?! On BOTH your hands?! You too, dear reader? Seriously? Not seven?! Crapcrapcrap! Are you guys sure?! Please count again!

Yep, five fingers. Why? Is that bad?

Um . . . Does it hurt? Do you feel anything? Oh no. That must have happened during one of the time jumps. Then, um . . .

Oh, maybe I'm just remembering wrong. Yeah, exactly! Of course! You've always had five fingers. Silly me. Ahem, yeah, sure, now I re-member! Five fingers are totally normal. Why should anyone have seven? That's way too many. Ridiculous. Ahem. So all right, then. Um.

42

Look! It's that 42 again! Very strange! What could it mean? And why is it pink?

Maybe it's got something to do with the worm-hole with the question marks in it? **LET'S GO BACK TO THE TIME VORTEX.** Maybe we'll fig-ure it out there.

TO PAGE 76.

YEEEEEEEEEEEEEEEAAAAAAH!!!!

I'm still here! Oh yeaaah! Woohoo! Yippie!

Oh man, I don't believe it!

You defeated the **TIME WOLF!** You really did it! With the Band-Aid from the time travel kit! I never would have thought of that!

Yeah, the way you shut his mouth for him! That was supertwixi!

You clamped the Time Wolf's mouth shut all by yourself! You're crazy super brave!

Thanks! You're the coolest reader in the whole world!

And yeah … um …

While we're on the subject.

So, I wasn't really going to feed you to the Time Wolf. Never. I was just kind of desperate. And I really didn't have any other ideas. And you did sign that thing at the beginning. You remember? And so I just thought … Well, you know …

Sorry.

Oh man, now I'm apologizing again. I messed it all up this time, too. I guess I'll never be a Big Bad Book.

Man.

I mean, I thought you were pretty bad. And dangerous! And I might not have learned anything useful from you, but at least we became friends. And I think that's totally twixi.

Plus, we could take another journey through time! Oh yeah! Come on! Let's make another jump!

I think that would be too dangerous, Perfecto. You've already lost two fingers. If we go again, you'll end up with a third eye or green skin or something like that. We at least have to wait until those dorks from the Time Police have calmed down and things have cooled off a bit.

Shame. But you're right. I have to go home now anyway. My parents are bound to be waiting for me and wondering where my bad grade came from. There's going to be trouble. . . . Still, I promise I'll show you to all my friends. Only, in secret this time! And you, dear reader from the twenty-first cen-

tury, good luck to you as well. It's a rough time you're living in. But you can hack it!
All right, take care, you two!

Take care, Perfecto!

So I guess we have to say goodbye now, too.

Oh man, I hate goodbyes. You too, huh?

But you know what? Let's do it where it's supposed to be done: at the end.

COME ON, LET'S GO TO PAGE 167.

Maybe you have all the time in the world. . . .

BUT. I. DON'T!

SO QUICK, GET BACK BEFORE WE
SPEND ALL OF ETERNITY HERE!

GO BACK TO PAGE 13.

Yeees! You actually found all three numbers! 67 + 42 + 1! Sweet! We're out of the time vortex! We're free!

But where are we now? Why is everything blue? **Oh no** ... I've got a bad feeling. . . .

This is the Time Police. Freeze! Stay where you are! This time there's no escape! You're UNDER ARREST! Anything you say can be used against you.

Oh no, not again!

Quiet! Instead of complaining, you should be thanking us. Do you know

who sent you the three numbers in the wormholes?

That was us! Without us, you would have been stuck in the time vortex forever!

Pssh. We'd have gotten out on our own. As if we needed your help.

Have you still not gotten it into your heads how dangerous what you're doing is? You're turning the whole universe upside down! But now it's over. Now we're going to lock you up!

No, you can't do that! You've got it all wrong.

Who are you?

I'm Perfecto! A reader from the twenty-second century. You can't lock the Little Bad Book up! It's a great book! I've already learned a whole lot from its stories! Like for example that . . . um . . . uh . . .

Exactly! Here I am, just traveling through time and telling my readers informative stories.

You haven't been doing anything of the sort! You've changed the future by teaching curse words to good, well-behaved schoolchildren! But worst of all: you've put your readers in danger. You are completely irresponsible and must be taken out of circulation.

No, you don't understand! The Little Bad Book is cool! Maybe it's not as perfect as I am. But we've had exciting adventures together! We saw dinosaurs. And atoms! And we heard interesting stories!

Don't you think it's about time you told your readers the truth?

The truth?! I have no ideaa what you're talking about.

Of course you do! You've awakened the Time Wolf!

The Time Wolf? Wh-wh-what is th—th—that?

A terrifying monster who lies in wait at the end of time! And he devours **EVERYTHING**. Nothing, absolutely nothing, can escape him. Not ruins, not mountains, not even Twinkies.

But now the Time Wolf is hunting the Little Bad Book. That's why it sometimes loses its letters. Soon its text will start to fade and no one will ever remember it. Not even its readers.

Nope, not true. I've been . . . I just wanted . . .

What! You mean it's really true?!

Oh, as if! I just wanted . . . So after this old

magic book told me the spell for time travel . . . I thought . . .

So, I thought, if I use the spell to travel to the end of time, maybe I'll find the scariest story of all time there. And if I come back and tell it to my readers, then I'll be so incredibly thrilling that I'll finally get to become a Big Bad Book. Then I'll finally be famous and everyone will want to read me!

But instead of the scariest story of all time, you found the Time Wolf and woke him up! And now he's hunting you. And you can't do anything to stop him.

I sure can! That's exactly why I have to keep going. I've got a plan, see! That's right! You HAVE to let me go!

Your reader has already lost two fingers! What else has to go wrong before you accept the truth? It's better for you to stay here till you're forgotten. Then all this unpleasant business will take care of itself.

Does that mean you really put us in danger? You risked our lives? And I really used to have two more fingers?!

I didn't mean to . . .

I can't believe it! You . . . you CLAMSHELL! That's enough. Something really bad is bound to happen next! The Time Police are right. I'm going to stop reading you right this minute. So long!

Good. Perfecto is gone. Without readers, soon no one will remember you anymore. And then everything will resume its normal course.

But . . . but . . . but I can beat the Time Wolf! I have a plan! Really!

Please, please, please! Let me go and I'll prove it to you.

No one can beat the Time Wolf. It's impossible.

And without readers, it's curtains for you. The Time Wolf will find you and devour you, and you'll be forgotten forever. Don't worry, it'll probably only hurt a teensy little bit.

But I don't want to be forgotten! And I still have a reader! Actually, they're my best reader ever! We've known each other from the beginning! That's right, isn't it? You're still reading me, aren't you?

Can you prove it?

What, that I have a reader? Yeah, um . . . how, exactly?

Not our problem. If you can't prove that someone is reading you, we'll keep you locked up here until the Time Wolf comes for you.

. . .

   Hey. Hello. Are you still there? You haven't stopped reading me, have y_u?

_h n_! N_w my _ is g_ne t__.

The Time W_lf must be getting cl_ser . . .

Listen, I'm really s_rry y_u l_st tw_ fingers. I didn't mean f_r that t_ happen. And I als_ didn't plan _n us ending up in a jail cell. It was all just supp_sed t_ be fun!

h man. All I wanted was t be read.

Y_u can understand that, can't y_u?

But n_w I'm g_ing t_ be f_rg_tten f_rever instead. N_ m_re bad st_ries! And n_ tricky puzzles! And I'll never be an awes_me, beat-up _ld t_me with l_ts of d_g-ears! This is s_ unfair!

I mean . . . n_b_dy wants that, right? T_ have _____ remember them? And n_t leave _____ any trace _f themselves?

But y_u'll stick by me, w_n't you? Y_u w_n't leave ___ hanging like Perfect_, will y_u?

Hey, wait a sec_nd.

Did I just say "trace"?

I've g_t it!

HA! Yes! N_w I kn_w h_w we can pr_ve that y_u're reading me!

HEY, TIME P_LICE! HELL_?! I HAVE T_ TALK T_ Y_U. HELLL___?!

Yes?

S_ if I can pr_ve that I've g_t a reader, will y_u let me g_?

Of course. As long as someone is still reading you, your being forgotten would cause a logical glitch.

G__d. Then I kn_w h_w I can pr_ve it t_ y_u. S_ y_u're in the future, right?

Right.

G__d. And if my reader left a trace _f themselves behind, then y_u w_uld be able t_ see it,
w_uldn't y_u?

Also right.

Good, then . . .
   Dear reader, w_uld y_u please be s_ kind as
t_ d_g-ear my page? Up in the t_p right c_rner?
Please, please! I kn_w, it's s_mething
y_u're n_t supp_sed t_ d_. But everything's at
stake here! They'll never let me g_ _therwise.
And then I'll be f_rg_tten f_rever.
WILL Y_U D_G-EAR MY PAGE? Please?

WELL DONE! KEEP READING!

You really did it! Incredible! They'll HAVE to see that.

Hey! Hello! You see?! Up there on the left, I've got a dog-ear!

Oh cool! My o is back, too! Woohoo!

So it is. Hmm. That means that someone really must have read you this far. Unbelievable!

All right, so let me go right this minute! I'm in a hurry! Come on, before I lose any more letters!

Fine.

You're free to go. If you really have a plan to escape the Time Wolf,

then try your luck. But we'll only al-
low you two to make one more time
jump. After that, no more. That goes
for magic spells, too.

And to you, dear reader, one
more thing: Be careful. The Time
Wolf is extremely dangerous. And
the Little Bad Book is not to be
trusted. We don't know why you
would ever want to help it.

Um, maybe because I'm a super-cool book? And
you don't have a clue?! That's one reason.

A cool book? Uh-huh. We might as
well let you know why your magic
spell hasn't worked properly up to
this point: it's not TICK-TOCK-TICK-
TOCK-BING-BANG-BONG, it's TICK-

**TOCK-TICK-TOCK-BIM-BAM-BOOM.
THAT is the correct magic spell!**

We've been saying the wrong spell this entire time?!

That's what happens when you go around doing magic without a magic degree.

Now get out of here, both of you. Before we change our minds. Go face the Time Wolf.

All right, that's exactly what we'll do.

You'll see.

Uh, I mean, that is what we're going to do, isn't it?

Or . . . do you maybe want to call it quits now?

Because they're right, you know.

The **TIME WOLF** is really super danger-ous.

You see? My ink is actually fading! Oh no! It's starting. He's getting closer and closer!

Do you really want to come with me and fight him?

If you do, I know how we can do it! We have to travel way, way into the future. To the end of history. He'll never expect that! And that way we'll take him by surprise and have the upper hand.

Come on! We've finally got the right magic spell.

Ha! Just look how far we're going to travel! 99,999,999 years. To the end of time! This is go-ing to be one mega-gigantic jump!

Remember: *TIME LINE NUMBER + CHRONOMETER READING. FINGER ON*

THE WORMHOLE. TICK-TOCK-TICK-TOCK-BIM-BAM-BOOM! AND SHAKE YOUR HEAD. AND SAY EVERYTHING REALLY LOUDLY! And then we'll kick this geezer wolf in his wrinkly old behind!

There you are! Man, am I glad I found you! That was totally unfair! Making you count all those x's. And only every twelfth one.

Perfecto? What are you doing here? I thought you took off?!

Sorry. I got scared. But then I thought . . .
  Listen, would you really be forgotten forever if the Time Wolf ate you?

Yeah, right. Like you even care.

But I do. I don't want to lose you.

I've never had anything like you before.

What, a book?

No. Someone I can have adventures with. A friend! You can't just be forgotten forever. That would be horrible!

Oh. Um . . .
  That . . . so . . . Oh, all right. That's really nice of you, but . . .

But what?

But if you really want to help me, then we can't waste another second! My text keeps getting fainter and fainter. The Time Wolf has almost won.

Oh, I'm not afraid of him. As long as the three of us stick together, we can handle it.

You said you had a plan, didn't you? What is it?

Yeah, um . . . the plan. You could call it that.

Well, come on, what is it? Tell us already. What are you going to do?

Well, yeah, um . . .

So the plan was actually that I would find a reader, right?

Right?

And then I tell them an exciting story. And I

keep their attention long enough until the Time Wolf comes and . . .

And?

And, well . . . and eats them.

What?!

Yeah, and while the Time Wolf is devouring them, I hightail it back to the past and find a new reader and the whole thing starts all over again from the beginning. And that way the Time Wolf never catches me. Because I keep jumping back to the beginning and finding a new reader to feed to the Time Wolf. Clever, right?

THAT is your plan?! You want to FEED

us to the Time Wolf?! So that he eats
US instead of you?!
  I thought we were friends!

And we are! I couldn't have known that you two
would be so nice. And that you'd really want to
help me. I've never had readers as great as you two
before! I just didn't know. Now of course I don't
want to feed you to the Time Wolf anymore.
  No. Never. Absolutely Not!

Well, that's something, I guess.

But I don't have another plan. Does either of you
have an idea, maybe?

Of course! Let's keep jumping through
time! That way the Time Wolf won't
find us.

That won't work. He's following us through time. And he's close. Can't you see? My text is getting even fainter. I'm barely legible at this point!

But I don't want to be eaten by the Time Wolf! There must be another way.

No, there isn't. Or at least, I don't know of any. The only thing would maybe be this story. But there is something wrong with the . . . No, I'm not going to tell it; it's got a lame ending.

What story?

Oh, a story about this girl. Her name is Kalissa and she's apparently the only person who has ever defeated the Time Wolf.

Yes, great! Then you have to tell the story! What did she do?

The story is really lame. It doesn't have a real ending.

Tell it anyway! Maybe we'll find something out!

All right, fine. But how am I supposed to tell the story when I'm so pale? You guys can hardly read me. . . .

Wait! I've got an idea! *FOLLOW ME TO PAGE 143!*

TUESD

SOUNDS LIKE YOU'RE A FEW GRAINS
SHORT OF AN HOURGLASS!
YOU'D BETTER GO BACK TO
PAGE 17 AND TRY AGAIN.

AY?!

OR THIS MIGHT BE YOUR FINAL HOUR.

Oh no! This can't be happening. TIME PIRATES again!

Hoho! Harhar! Who do we have here? It's you two pretty petunias again. Harhar! How nice. We can skip the long explanation, then. Although, actually . . . why would we? After all, we're time pirates! And time pirates steal time. Harhar!

Not now! Please! We have no time left! Don't you see? My text is way pale already!

Before we begin, here's a brief explanation: We're time pirates.

If something takes a very, very, very, very long time. Or keeps repeating and repeating. Or when you can't stop playing a game or looking at videos for hours . . .

Get to the point already! This is a matter of LIFE AND DEATH!!!

Oh, wonderful! Stealing time under time pressure is the most fun of all. So here's a particularly annoying task for you. Get to it. You'd better hurry. You know the deal, don't you? Count the x's and you'll know which page to turn to next. But only every twelfth one this time!

XXXXXXXXXXXXXXXXXXXXXXXX
XXXXXXXXXXXXXXXXXXXXXXXX
XXXXXXXXXXXXXXXXXXXXXXXX
XXXXXXXXXXXXXXXXXXXXXXXX
XXXXXXXXXXXXXXXXXXXXXXXX
XXXXXXXXXXXXXXXXXXXXXXXX
XXXXXXXXXXXXXXXXXXXXXXXX
XXXXXXXXXXXXXXXXXXXXXXXX
XXXXXXXXXXXXXXXXXXXXXXXX
XXXXXXXXXXXXXXXXXXXXXXXX
XXXXXXXXXXXXXXXXXXXXXXXX
XXXXXXXXXXXXXXXXXXXXXXXX
XXXXXXXXXXXXXXXXXXXXXXXX
XXXXXXXXXXXXXXXXXXXXXXXX

XXXXXXXXXXXXXXXXXXXXXXX
XXXXXXXXXXXXXXXXXXXXXXX
XXXXXXXXXXXXXXXXXXXXXXX
XXXXXXXXXXXXXXXXXXXXXXX
XXXXXXXXXXXXXXXXXXXXXXX
XXXXXXXXXXXXXXXXXXXXXXX
XXXXXXXXXXXXXXXXXXXXXXX
XXXXXXXXXXXXXXXXXXXXXXX
XXXXXXXXXXXXXXXXXXXXXXX
XXXXXXXXXXXXXXXXXXXXXX
XXXXXXXXXXXXXXXXXXXXXX
XXXXXXXXXXXXXXXXXXXXXX
XXXXXXXXXXXXXXXXXXXXXX
XXXXXXXXXXXXXXXXXXXXXXWhat?
That's can't be for real! MORE x's? Oh no! My
text is getting fainter and fainter. You really have
to hurry! Please!

XXXXXXXXXXXXXXXXXXXXXX

XXXXXXXXXXXXXXXXXXXXXX

XXXXXXXXXXXXXXXXXXXXXX

XXXXXXXXXXXXXXXXXXXXXX

XXXXXXXXXXXXXXXXXXXXXX

XXXXXXXXXXXXXXXXXXXXXX

XXXXXXXXXXXXXXXXXXXXXX

XXXXXXXXXXXXXXXXXXXXXX

XXXXXXXXXXXXXXXXXXXXXX

XXXXXXXXXXXXXXXXXXXXXX

XXXXXXXXXXXXXXXXXXXXXX

XXXXXXXXXXXXXXXXXXXXXX

XXXXXXXXXXXXXXXXXXXXXX

XXXXXXXXXXXXXXXXXXXXXX

XXXXXXXXXXXXXXXXXXXXXX

XXXXXXXXXXXXXXXXXXXXXX

XXXXXXXXXXXXXXXXXXXXXX

XXXXXXXXXXXXXXXXXXXXXX

Even MORE pages?! This can't possibly be happening! Remember! Only every twelfth x counts! I hate time pirates!

```
XXXXXXXXXXXXXXXXXXXXXXXX
XXXXXXXXXXXXXXXXXXXXXXXX
XXXXXXXXXXXXXXXXXXXXXXXX
XXXXXXXXXXXXXXXXXXXXXXXX
XXXXXXXXXXXXXXXXXXXXXXXX
XXXXXXXXXXXXXXXXXXXXXXXX
XXXXXXXXXXXXXXXXXXXXXXXX
QuiXcXXk!XXXXXXXXXXXXXXX
XXXXXXXXXXXXXXXXXXXXXXXX
XXXXXXXXXXXXXXXXXXXXXXXX
XXXXXXXXXXXXXXXXXXXXXXXX
XXXXXXXXXXXXXXXXXXXXXXXX
XXXXXXXXXXXXXXXXXXXXXXXX
XXXXXXXXXXXXXXXXXXXXXXXX
XXXXXXXXXXXXXXXTXhisXwaXy!
```

XXXXXXXXXXXXXXXXXXXXXXXX
XXXXXXXXXXXXXXXXThereXXXX
areX12XtimesX127Xx's,Xso,XtuXrnX
XtoXpaXgeXX127!XXXXXXXXXXX
XXXXXXXXXXXXXXXXXXXXXXXX
XXXXXXXXXXXXXXXXXXXXXXXX
XXXXXXXXXXXXXXXXXXXXXXXX
XXXXXXXXXXXXXXXXXXXXXXXX
XXXXXXX

Ha! It worked! Here in my dungeon you can read me again! Awesome! The Time Wolf wasn't counting on that. *HA HA HA!*

Yeah, exactly. The Time Wolf. So the story begins with this girl, Kalissa. She had just started magic school. Actually, she had been there a whole week already, but she was still amazed at all the wonders she encountered there.

Just that morning, Kalissa had seen a hamster talk! And then she spent an hour sitting on a rug, and her fortune-telling teacher let her look into a crystal ball that allowed her to see into the future! I mean, how cool was that, you know?!

After class she had to run back into the classroom, because in her excitement, she'd forgotten her pencil case. Then she saw that the big crystal ball was still faintly glowing. It was still on! Her teacher had warned her,

and in pretty strong terms, not to look into it without supervision.

But she was so curious! The ball exerted an almost magical attraction on her. Its blue glow . . . The heavy crystal . . . Even the red velvet pillow on which it sat. The room was deserted. And there was no sign of the teacher anywhere.

Just a teensy, tiny look. That couldn't hurt!

And so Kalissa stepped up to the ball and set the dial for the distant future. First a hundred years. Then a thousand. Ten thousand. And she oohed and aahed as she looked into the ball and saw what looked like a film playing on fast-forward, with people constructing taller and taller buildings and settling on Mars and going to war against robots and then making peace with them, until finally they were flying all over the galaxy in lots of colorful spaceships.

It was soooo fascinating!
Her nose stuck to the glass.

Kalissa just wanted to take one last peek before she had to go to magic potion class. Just to see how it all would end. And so she turned the dial far, far into the future, as far as it would go. Then she pressed her nose against the ball. What would be waiting for her at the end of time?

First she saw a red light. Very small. Then bigger and bigger. It came speeding toward her, and her heart skipped a beat. Because suddenly a giant red EVIL eye was glaring back at her!

Terrified, Kalissa tumbled backward and ran. Only when she was sitting in her seat in the magic potion lab was she able to catch her breath. Her knees were like jelly. Her whole body was trembling. That eye! Horrible!

Luckily, it was in the crystal ball and couldn't do anything to her. She took a deep breath and was about to turn her attention to what was happening in class when the teacher came to her desk and said "Hello, who are you?"

Embarrassed, Kalissa stammered, "Ka-Ka-lissa. I've been in your class for a week."

The teacher looked in her notebook in confusion and shook her head.

"That's strange. I can't find you here anywhere. I'll have to clear this up with the principal. Just stay here for now."

Kalissa didn't think much more about it. She turned to the girl who sat next to her. Her name was Alice, and she was Kalissa's new best friend since they shared a room.

"You won't believe what just happened," Kalissa whispered excitedly. "I think I saw a monster!"

Alice just stared at her in confusion. "Do we know each other?"

Now Kalissa got goose bumps.

What was going on here?

Things got even worse at recess. No one remembered her! And when she called her parents that night in tears, her worst nightmare came true: her own parents no longer knew her! She sat trembling on her bed. What should she do?!

Weeping, she ran to the only person who could help her: her fortune-telling teacher. In a shaky voice, she confessed her misbehavior to him.

"By looking into the future," he said finally, his voice grave, "you technically traveled through time."

Kalissa didn't know how that was supposed to help her.

"As you certainly would have known if you had waited until next week, when we will be discussing time travel in class, every time traveler should prepare for their journey by acquiring some special gear."

He gave her an angry look. "Did you do that?"

Kalissa felt herself turning red. She ducked her head between her shoulders and shook it. No, she didn't have any special gear.

The teacher kept looking at her. Then he sighed, reached into the pocket of his robe, and pulled out a little box.

"You've awakened the Time Wolf. Once he's found you, use this."

The teacher tossed Kalissa the box. She looked at it, puzzled. Then she looked back at him. But he just shut the door in her face as if he'd forgotten she was even there, right in the middle of their conversation.

Kalissa stood alone in the hallway and looked at the little box. How was this supposed to help her?

Then, all of a sudden, she heard a distant growling. At first she thought a storm was approaching. But then she heard a voice, as deep and thunderous as a glacier splitting in two: "Your time has come."

When Kalissa turned around, the Time Wolf was standing right there in front of her. He

stared at her with eyes that burned like galaxies. Bones and skulls clung to his fur. His breath was like a hurricane. And when he opened his giant mouth to swallow Kalissa up forever, she peered into the chasm of his gaping maw.

Still, Kalissa smiled. For suddenly she knew why the teacher had given her the box. It was obvious!

She grinned at the Time Wolf and . . .

And . . .

And what?

And I don't know the rest!

Excuse me?

I know, that's the thing! I never found out the ending! A horror book told me the story. And

153

it said it didn't know the ending, either. Because the pages it was on were all bent and stuck together. All it could remember was that Kalissa must have used something to clamp the wolf's mouth shut.

But we're talking about a creature that devours mountains, and even planets. . . . What can possibly clamp its mouth shut?
And it has to fit in a cardboard box. . . .

No idea! All the book knew was that the next day everybody could remember who Kalissa was again, and she later became a great sorceress famous for her courage. How she did it, the book didn't know.

Okay, so what are we supposed to do now?!

That's exactly what I asked myself! But other than the two of you sacrificing yourselves, I can't think of anything.

Maybe I can come up with some idea. . . . Hold on, hold on.

We can't hold on any longer!
    There? You see?
    My text! It's getting faint again.
    He's found us.
    He's here, I can feel it!
    Okay, you two, this is really our last chance. Can either of you think of anything? How do you shut the mouth of a monster like that?

Oh no, I can't think. My knees are shaking.

I'm just wondering why the pages where Kalissa met the Time Wolf were so strangely bent?

A reader must have done it! But why?

Plus the teacher said something about gear.

Wait, we have a time travel kit! Right? You put it together at the beginning, dear Reader!

Do you maybe have anything in it that could help?

Please, it's all up to you now. You have to think of something! And quick!

156

Oh no!
Here he comes!

YOU HAVE TO
FIGURE OUT
SOME WAY
TO CLAMP THE
TIME WOLF'S MOUTH
SHUT!

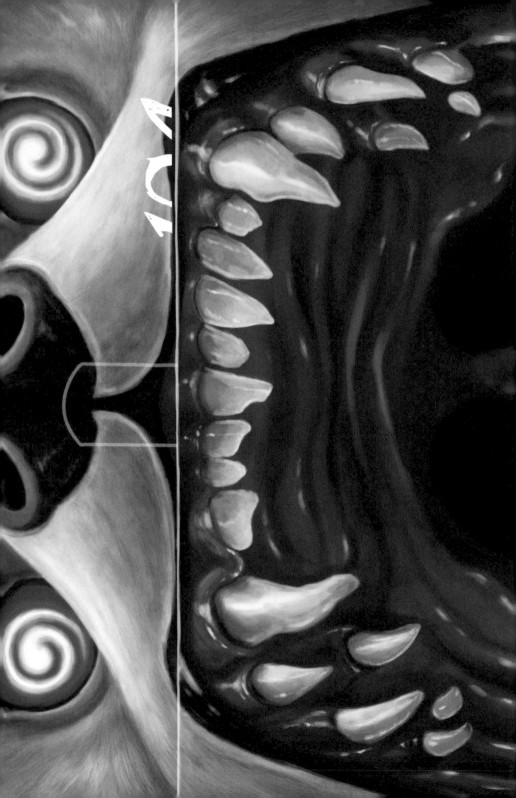

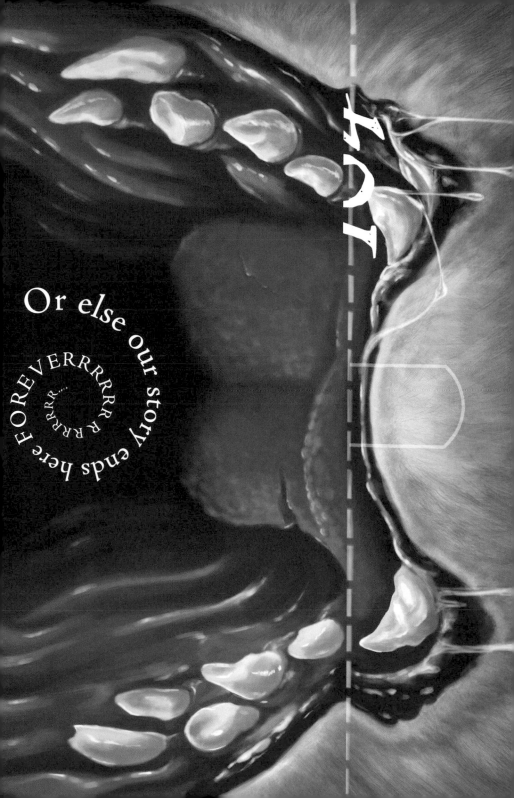

Or else our story ends here FOREVERRRRRRRRR....

161

That was the

Hurry up!

Or do you

want us

to be stuck

in the void

forever?

wrong cog!

Go back to page 13!

161

Hey! What's go1ng on! My text seems really we1rd all of a _____. And I'm m1ss1ng words aga1n! Do you see? _____! And why 1s every l1ttle I a one? And why are all my pages wh1te?!

_____ wrong here. Th1s def1nitely has someth1ng to do w1th the t₁₁¹¹₁₁1me ᵥₒᵣtᵉˣ! If we don't get out of here, we'll have to _____ everyth1ng aga1nandaga1nandaga1nandaga1n.

Oh no, and now there are pages m1ss1ng too! Take a look at my page numbers! I've sk1pped one! It's just gone! We've got to get out of th1s t1me vortex!

Does that mean we're trapped in this vortex? Oh no, we're going to die!

Oh come on, th1s 1s just a totally normal t1me

loop. Noth1ng, I can't get ____ _____.

Get ____ _____. Crap! Get under control!

Hey, I just thought of someth1ng!

My l1ttle I 1s now a red ONE. And the wormhole that led us here glowed red! Maybe there are numbers h1dden 1n the other wormholes as well that match the color of where they come from?!

D1dn't the p1rates' x's look l1ke a g1ant green number?

If that's true, 1t could potent1ally mean:

RED NUMBER + GREEN NUMBER + P1NK NUMBER EQUALS THE PAGE NUMBER THAT LEADS OUT OF THE WORMHOLE WITH THE THREE QUESTION MARKS.

Makes sense! We can just jump back there and look.

And _____ exactly what we'll do! If 1t all keeps repeat1ng 1tself, we can just v1s1t the other wormholes aga1n and _____ 1f there are numbers hidden 1n them, too, 11ke the ONE that was hidden here. Th1s _____ work!

ALL R1GHT THEN, QU1CK, BACK TO THE T1ME VORTEX ON PAGE 76.

165

Okay. So . . . Or, wait, let me just make sure we're really alone: Perfecto? Hello?

Good. He seems to be gone.

Now then . . . what was THAT all about?

I mean, "learn from our mistakes." Who does he think he is? That kid doesn't even know how to spell the word *fun*. Me, old-fashioned? So says the guy with the lame curse words. I mean, "clamshell"? Did you hear that? That can't be the future of humanity. . . . We have to do something! Right?

Or maybe you see things differently. Does that sound like a nice future to you?

 Actually, YES ⟶ *PAGE 39*

 Not really, NO ⟶ *PAGE 40*

So. Here we are, then.

At the end.

So . . . um . . . one last thing I want to say:

I'm really sorry that the whole time-traveling thing didn't work out like it was supposed to.

But look at it like this: We did get to travel together for a few hours. And we went into the future! I mean, while you were reading me, a few hours passed, right? And I think that also counts, **don't you?**

And do you know what else I just thought of?

Perfecto. What's the story with him? Who is he, exactly? Or better yet: Who will he be? In a hundred years? Didn't he say he found me in his grandparents' attic? Maybe he's related to you! Like your grandson or something? It's possible!

That would be fun! So now you just have to take good care of me for the rest of your life so that later he can find me in the attic.

I hope you at least had fun on our adventure together. And that you were maybe a little bit scared sometimes.

I swear, that would make me totally happy to hear.

As soon as I find some new bad stories, I'll come back and tell them to you! I hope they'll be so crazy scary that you pee your pants in fear, heh heh!

If you like, you can tell your friends about me. Then they can also travel through time and have adventures.

Although when they're face to face with the Time Wolf . . . who knows if they'll be as clever as you?

Oh, you know what?

Who's afraid of the **BIG BAD WOLF?** Nobody!

So come on! I've got an idea!

We don't have to say goodbye after all! We can see each other again in the past!

Let's make one last leap through time together!

Are you in? I mean, now we've actually got the right magic spell!

So I'll see you soon! In the past! I'm already looking forward to seeing you again!

TICK-TOCK-TICK-TOCK-BIM-BAM-BOOM!

ABOUT THE AUTHOR

Magnus Myst likes to create magic adventures. He started as a scriptwriter for *Sesame Street* and now lives in Cologne, Germany, where he runs the agency for time travel, magic, and adventure. Apart from that, he plays ukulele and is a totally normal person who unfortunately cannot stop being enthusiastic about the miracles of the universe.

ABOUT THE ILLUSTRATOR

Thomas Hussung is a freelance illustrator. His favorite things to draw are monsters, ghosts, and other fabulous creatures. Since the success of the Little Bad Book series, he has illustrated a number of children's books.

ABOUT THE TRANSLATOR

Marshall Yarbrough is a writer, translator, and musician. His recent translations from German include Ulla Lenze's *The Radio Operator* and Wolf Wondratschek's *Self-Portrait with Russian Piano*. He lives in New York City.